The Golden Egg Book

By Margaret Wise Brown

Pictures by Lilian Obligado

A GOLDEN BOOK • NEW YORK
Western Publishing Company, Inc.
Racine, Wisconsin 53404

Once there was a little bunny.
He was all alone.
One day he found an egg.
He could hear something moving
inside the egg.
What was it?

Maybe a little boy,

Maybe an elephant,

Maybe another bunny,

Maybe a mouse.

Who could tell what he would find?
And how would a little bunny know?
But there was something inside that egg.

He could hear something moving.
He shook it.

Then the bunny
pushed the egg
with his foot.

He jumped on top of the egg.

He climbed a tree and threw nuts at it.

He rolled the egg down a hill.
But still the egg shell didn't break.
And whatever was in the egg
didn't come out.

So the bunny threw a rock at the egg.
But because he was only a little bunny, it
was a very little rock and he didn't throw
it very hard and the egg didn't break.

Pick Pick Pick.
Something was trying to get out of that egg.
The bunny sat very still and watched through
his shining eyes.

He sat very still and listened with his
big soft ears.
Pick Pick Pick.

Then the little bunny
began to yawn.

And he yawned
and he yawned.

The egg was very quiet.

He curled up all sleepy and warm
close to the egg and went to sleep.
He went to sleep because he was
so sleepy.
Then . . .

Pick Pick Pick
and Peck Peck Peck
And crackety CRACK!
Out jumped a little yellow duck.

"Well, what is this?" said the little duck
when he saw the bunny.
"What could this little fur thing be?"

The bunny was very sleepy,
so he was still asleep
and didn't wake up.

"Inside the egg,"
said the duck,
"I thought I was all alone
in a small dark world."

"Now I find myself alone with a bunny
in a big bright world.
And the bunny won't wake up."

So the duck pushed the bunny
with his foot

And jumped on top of him
And threw a little rock at him

And rolled him down a hill.

And the bunny woke up.
"Where is my egg?" said the bunny.
"And where did you come from?"

"Never mind that," said the duck.
"Here I am."
So the bunny and the duck were friends,
And no one was ever alone again.